# Usborne
# Phonics Readers
# Toad makes a road

Phil Roxbee Cox
Illustrated by Stephen Cartwright
Edited by Jenny Tyler

Language consultant: Marlynne Grant
BSc, CertEd, MEdPsych, PhD, AFBPs, CPsychol

There is a little yellow duck to find on every page.

First published in 2006 by Usborne Publishing Ltd., Usborne House, 83-85 Saffron Hill, London EC1N 8RT, England. www.usborne.com
Copyright © 2006, 2000 Usborne Publishing Ltd.

Toad hops happily.
She has a new house on the hill.

"My new house is best," she boasts.

3

Toad waits and waits for the truck to bring her things.

She's in luck.
There's the truck.

"I can't get up the hill. The load will spill."

There's no track for the truck.

So, Toad brings her things up the hill.

Toad is tired.
  With one last hop
    she flops into bed...

Next day, Toad eats toast.
"Today is my party!"

But only Billy the goat gets up the hill.

"It's far too steep,
except for me
or a sheep."

"What you need
is a road, Toad."

"If I need a road, then I'll make a road!" says Toad.

But toads can't make roads,"
says Billy. "That's silly."

Wait and see!"
says Toad.

Toad clears a track.

She lays black,
sticky tar.